This book, specially designed for young children, is a brief retelling of the famous story entitled *Peter Pan and Wendy*. When the children are a little older, they will want to read, as their fathers and mothers did, the whole story, many times longer than this, just as it was written by J. M. Barrie. Charles Scribner's Sons are the sole publishers of the complete and unabridged text, with pictures by Trina Schart Hyman.

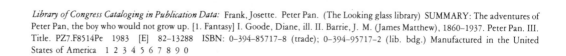

Library of Congress Cataloging in Publication Data: Frank, Josette. Peter Pan. (The Looking glass library) SUMMARY: The adventures of Peter Pan, the boy who would not grow up. [1. Fantasy] I. Goode, Diane, ill. II. Barrie, J. M. (James Matthew), 1860–1937. Peter Pan. III. Title. PZ7.F8514Pe 1983 [E] 82–13288 ISBN: 0–394–85717–8 (trade); 0–394–95717–2 (lib. bdg.) Manufactured in the United States of America 1 2 3 4 5 6 7 8 9 0

PETER PAN

BY J. M. BARRIE
ILLUSTRATED BY DIANE GOODE

Edited by Josette Frank from *Peter Pan and Wendy*

A LOOKING GLASS LIBRARY BOOK

Random House 🏠 New York

The Darling family lived at number 14. There were Mr. and Mrs. Darling and their three children. Wendy was the oldest, then came John, then little Michael. There was nothing out of the ordinary about the Darling family; they were just like any of the other families that lived on their street, except for one thing. They employed a big Newfoundland dog as a nursemaid for their children. She was called Nana. The Darlings had found her in Kensington Gardens.

Mrs. Darling always said that Nana was a "treasure"; but Mr. Darling was a little afraid the neighbors might think it odd to have a dog for a nurse. Nana loved the children dearly and took the best care of them, giving them their baths and making sure they took their medicine. Of course, her kennel was in the nursery, and she was up at any moment of the night if one of her charges made the slightest cry.

There was never a simpler, happier family, until the coming of Peter Pan. That was the night on which the extraordinary adventures of these children began.

It happened to be Nana's evening off, and Mrs. Darling had bathed the children and tucked them snugly into their beds. One by one they had slid into the land of sleep. Then Mrs. Darling had sat down by the fire to sew. But the fire was warm and the lights were dim, and soon her head was nodding and she, too, was asleep.

She was having a troubled dream about her children when the window of the nursery blew open and a boy dropped quietly to the floor. At the same time a strange light, no bigger than a child's fist, darted about the room like a living thing. It must have been this light that awakened Mrs. Darling. She started up with a cry and saw the boy. He was a lovely boy, clad in skeleton leaves and the juices that ooze out of trees. When he saw that Mrs. Darling was a grownup, he gnashed his teeth at her.

Mrs. Darling screamed, and, as if in answer to a bell, the door opened and Nana entered, returning from her night out. She growled and sprang at the boy, who leaped lightly through the window. Again Mrs. Darling screamed, this time in distress for him. She thought he must have been killed, for the nursery was on the third floor. She ran down into the street to look for him, but he was not there. She looked up, and in the black night she could see nothing but what she thought was a shooting star.

She returned to the nursery and found Nana with something in her mouth which proved to be the boy's shadow. For, as he had jumped, Nana had closed the window quickly. She had been too late

to catch him, but his shadow had not had time to get out. Slam went the window, and the shadow was left behind.

Nana had no doubt of what was the best thing to do with this shadow. She hung it out of the window, meaning "He is sure to come back for it; let us put it where he can get it easily without disturbing the children."

But unfortunately Mrs. Darling could not leave it hanging out of the window; it looked so like the washing. She decided to roll it up and put it carefully in a drawer until a fitting opportunity came to tell her husband about it. Ah me! The opportunity came a week later, on that never-to-be-forgotten Friday.

That Friday evening had begun uneventfully, exactly like a hundred other evenings. It happened that Mr. and Mrs. Darling were going out to dinner. Nana had bathed the children and got them ready for bed, and they were playing happily in the nursery. Mrs. Darling had come in, wearing her white evening gown. She had dressed early because Wendy loved to see her in her evening gown. Suddenly Mr. Darling came rushing into the nursery with a crumpled tie in his hand.

"Why, what is the matter, Father dear?" Wendy asked.

"Matter!" he yelled. "This tie, it will not tie. Not around my neck! Around the bedpost, yes; twenty times! But around my neck, no!"

"Let me try, dear," said Mrs. Darling, and with her nice cool hands she tied his tie for him. Mr. Darling thanked her, at once forgot his rage, and in another moment was dancing around the room with Michael on his back.

When the romp was over, Mrs. Darling felt this was an opportunity to tell her husband about the boy. At first he pooh-poohed the story, but he became thoughtful when she showed him the shadow.

"It is nobody I know," he said, examining it carefully, "but he does look like a scoundrel."

They were still discussing it when Nana came in. Most unluckily she rubbed against Mr. Darling, covering his trousers with hair. He was very angry. Of course Mrs. Darling brushed him, but he began to talk again about its being a mistake to have a dog for a nurse. "I refuse to allow that dog in my nursery for an hour longer."

The children wept, and Nana ran to him beseechingly. But he waved her back. "The proper place for you is in the yard, and there you go to be tied up this instant."

"George, George," Mrs. Darling warned him. "Remember what I told you about that boy."

Alas, he would not listen. He was determined to show who was master in that house. He seized Nana roughly and dragged her from the nursery.

In the meantime Mrs. Darling had put the children to bed in unusual silence and lit their night-lights. They could hear Nana barking, and John whimpered, "It is because he is chaining her up in the yard." But Wendy was wiser.

"That is not Nana's unhappy bark," she said, little guessing what was about to happen. "That is her bark when she smells danger."

Danger!

Mrs. Darling quivered and went to the window. It was securely fastened. A nameless fear clutched at her heart and made her cry. "Oh, how I wish that I weren't going to a party tonight!"

Even Michael, already half asleep, knew that she was troubled, and he asked, "Can anything harm us, Mother, after the night-lights are lit?"

"Nothing, precious," she said. "They are the eyes a mother leaves behind her to guard her children."

She went from bed to bed, and little Michael threw his arms around her. "Mother," he cried, "I love you!" They were the last words she was to hear from him for a long time.

Come Away, Come Away!

For a moment after Mr. and Mrs. Darling left the house, the night-lights by the beds of the three children continued to burn clearly. Suddenly the lights blinked and then went out.

There was another light in the room now, a thousand times brighter than the night-lights. In no time it had been in all the drawers in the nursery, looking for Peter's shadow, and had rummaged the wardrobe and turned every pocket inside out. It was not really a light. It made this light by flashing very quickly, but when it came to rest you saw that it was a girl fairy, no larger than your hand. She was called Tinker Bell.

A moment after the fairy's entrance, the window was blown open by the breathing of the little stars, and Peter dropped in.

"Tinker Bell," he called softly, after making sure that the children were asleep. "Tink, where are you?" She was in a jug for the moment, and liking it extremely; she had never been in a jug before.

"Oh, do come out of that jug, and tell me, do you know where they put my shadow?"

The loveliest tinkle as of golden bells answered him. It is the fairy language. Tink said the shadow was in the big chest, and Peter jumped at the drawers, scattering their contents on the floor with both hands. In a moment he had found his shadow, and in his delight he forgot that he had shut Tinker Bell up in a drawer.

No doubt he thought that he and his shadow, when brought near each other, would join like drops of water, and when this didn't happen he was terribly upset. He tried to stick the shadow on with soap from the bathroom, but that also failed. Peter sat on the floor and cried.

His sobs woke Wendy, and she sat up in bed. She was not alarmed to see a stranger crying on the nursery floor.

"Boy," she said courteously, "why are you crying?"

Peter could be very polite too; he rose and bowed to her beautifully. Wendy was much pleased, and bowed beautifully to him from the bed.

"What's your name?" he asked.

"Wendy Moira Angela Darling," she replied. "What is your name?"

"Peter Pan."

"Is that all?"

"Yes," he said rather sharply.

She asked where he lived.

"Second to the right," said Peter, "and then straight on till morning."

"What a funny address!" Wendy said nicely. "Is that what they put on the letters?"

"Don't get any letters," he said contemptuously.

"But your mother gets letters?"

"Don't have a mother," he said.

"Oh, Peter, no wonder you were crying," she said, and got out of bed and ran to him.

"I wasn't crying about mothers," he said rather indignantly. "I was crying because I can't get my shadow to stick on. Besides, I wasn't crying."

"It has come off?"

"Yes."

"How awful," Wendy said. But she could not help smiling when she saw that he had been trying to stick it on with soap. How exactly like a boy!

Fortunately she knew exactly what to do. "I shall sew it on for you." And she got out her sewing box and started to sew the shadow to Peter's foot.

"I daresay it will hurt a little," she warned him.

"Oh, I won't cry," said Peter. And he clenched his teeth and did not cry, and soon his shadow was behaving properly, though it was still a little creased.

Now Peter jumped about in the wildest glee. He had already forgotten that he owed his joy to Wendy. He thought he had attached the shadow himself. "How clever I am," he crowed. "Oh, the cleverness of me!"

"Well," said Wendy indignantly, "if I am no use I can at least withdraw." And she sprang into bed and covered her face with the blankets.

"Wendy," said Peter, "don't withdraw." Then, when she showed no sign of coming out, he said, "Wendy, I think one girl is of more use than twenty boys."

"I think it's perfectly sweet of you," Wendy declared, "and I'll get up again." She sat on the side of the bed and said she would give him a kiss if he liked. Peter did not know what she meant, and he held out his hand.

"Surely you know what a kiss is?" she asked, aghast.

"I shall know when you give it to me," he replied stiffly, and not to hurt his feelings, Wendy took the thimble from her finger and gave it to him.

"Now," said he, "shall I give you a kiss?"

"If you please," she replied primly, and held her face toward him. But he merely dropped an acorn button into her hand. So she said nicely that she would wear his kiss on the chain around her neck. It was lucky that she did put it on that chain, for it was afterward to save her life.

Now Wendy asked Peter many questions, and his answers filled her with surprise. How strange that he didn't know how old he was! "I ran away the day I was born," he explained. "It was because I heard Father and Mother talking about what I was to be when I became a man." Then, with great passion: "I don't want ever to be a man! I want always to be a little boy and to have fun. So I ran away to Kensington Gardens and lived a long time among the fairies."

Oh, did he really know fairies? Wendy poured out questions about them. Peter told her about the beginning of fairies.

"You see, Wendy, when the first baby laughed for the first time, its laugh broke into a thousand pieces, and they all went skipping about, and that was the beginning of fairies. And so there ought to be one fairy for every boy and girl—but there isn't. Because every time a child says 'I don't believe in fairies,' there is a fairy somewhere that falls down dead."

Now suddenly it struck him that Tinker Bell was keeping very quiet. "I can't think where she's gone to," he said.

"Peter," cried Wendy, "you don't mean to tell me there is a fairy in this room!"

There was a faint sound, like the tinkle of bells. The sound came from the chest of drawers.

"I do believe I shut her up in the drawer!" Peter whispered. He let poor Tink out of the drawer, and she flew about the nursery screaming with fury. "You shouldn't say such things," said Peter. "Of course I'm very sorry, but how could I know you were in the drawer?"

There were some angry bell tinkles.

"What is she saying now, Peter?" Wendy asked.

"She is not very polite. She says you are a great ugly girl, and that she is my fairy." He tried to argue with Tink, but she disappeared into the bathroom.

Now Wendy plied Peter with more questions. "If you don't live in Kensington Gardens now, where do you live mostly?"

"With the lost boys."

"Who are they?"

"They are the children who fall out of their carriages when the nursemaid is looking the other way. If they aren't claimed in seven days they are sent far away to the Neverland. I'm captain."

"What fun it must be!" said Wendy.

"Yes," said Peter, "but we are rather lonely, for there are no girls. Girls, you know, are far too clever to fall out of their carriages."

This flattered Wendy immensely. "I think," she said, "it is perfectly lovely, the way you talk about girls, so you may give me a kiss." For the moment she had forgotten his ignorance about kisses.

"I thought you'd be wanting it back," Peter said, and offered to return the thimble.

"Oh dear," said Wendy, "I don't mean a kiss, I mean a thimble."

"What's that?"

"It's like this." She kissed him.

"Funny," said Peter gravely. "Now shall I give you a thimble?"

"If you wish to," said Wendy.

Peter thimbled her, and almost immediately she screeched.

"What is it, Wendy?"

"It was exactly as if someone were pulling my hair."

"That must have been Tink." And indeed Tink was darting about again, using offensive language.

"She says she will do that to you, Wendy, every time I give you a thimble."

Peter could not understand why, but Wendy understood. And she was slightly disappointed when Peter admitted that he had come to the nursery window not to see her but to listen to stories.

"None of the lost boys knows any stories," he said. "And oh, Wendy, your mother was telling such a lovely story about the prince who couldn't find the lady who wore the glass slipper."

"That was 'Cinderella,'" said Wendy excitedly, "and, Peter, he found her and they lived happily ever after."

Peter rose quickly from the floor and hurried to the window.

"Where are you going?" Wendy cried.

"To tell the other boys."

"Don't go, Peter," she begged. "I know lots of stories."

Now Peter came back, and there was a greedy look in his eyes. He gripped her and began to draw her toward the window. "Wendy, do come with me and tell the other boys."

"Oh dear, I can't. Think of Mummy! Besides, I can't fly."

"I'll teach you," Peter promised.

"Oh, how lovely to fly!"

"I'll teach you to jump on the wind's back, and then away we go."

"Oo!" Wendy exclaimed rapturously.

"Wendy, you could tuck us in at night. None of us has ever been tucked in at night. And you could darn our clothes and make pockets for us. None of us has any pockets."

How could she resist? "It's awfully fascinating!" she cried. "Would you teach John and Michael to fly too?"

"If you like," Peter said.

Wendy ran to John and Michael and shook them. "Wake up!" she cried. "Peter Pan has come and he's going to teach us to fly."

John rubbed his eyes and sat up. "I say, Peter, can you really fly?"

Instead of answering him, Peter flew around the room, stepping onto the mantelpiece on the way.

It looked delightfully easy and the children tried it, first from the floor and then from the beds, but they always went down instead of up.

"I say, how do you do it?" asked John, rubbing his knee.

"You just think lovely thoughts and they lift you up in the air," Peter told them. And he showed them again. But not one of them could fly an inch.

Of course, Peter had been fooling them, for no one can fly unless

the fairy dust has been blown on him. Fortunately, Peter had some on one of his hands, and he blew some on each of them. "Now just wriggle your shoulders this way," he said, "and let go."

They were all on their beds, and Michael let go first. Immediately he was borne across the room. "I flewed!" he screamed. Then John let go and met Wendy near the bathroom. "Look at me!" "Look at me!" Up and down they went and around and around.

"I say," cried John, "why shouldn't we all go out?" Of course it was to this that Peter had been luring them. Michael was ready. But Wendy hesitated.

"There are mermaids!" said Peter.

"Oo!" cried Wendy. "To see a mermaid!"

"And pirates," added Peter.

"Pirates!" cried John, seizing his Sunday hat. "Let us go at once."

It was just at this moment that Mr. and Mrs. Darling, coming home from the party, opened the street door. They would have reached the nursery in time had it not been that the little stars were watching them. Once again the stars blew the window open and the smallest star of all called out: "Beware, Peter!"

Then Peter knew that there was not a moment to lose.

"Come," he cried, and soared out at once into the night, followed by John and Michael and Wendy.

Mr. and Mrs. Darling and Nana rushed into the nursery, but they were too late. The birds had flown.

The Flight

"Second to the right, and straight on till morning."

That, Peter had told Wendy, was the way to the Neverland. But even birds could not have sighted it with these instructions. Peter, you see, just said anything that came into his head.

The children flew for a long time—they did not know how long. Sometimes it was dark and sometimes light. Sometimes they were very cold and sometimes too warm. Sometimes they knew they were flying over the sea. When they grew tired or sleepy, Peter showed them how to lie flat on a strong wind, and that was such a pleasant change that they tried it several times. Indeed they would have slept longer, but Peter tired quickly of sleeping, and soon he would cry in his captain voice, "We get off here." With so little sleep, they were weary as they drew near the Neverland.

"There it is," said Peter calmly.

"Where, where?" the children wanted to know.

"Where all the arrows are pointing."

And indeed a million golden arrows were pointing out the island to the children, all directed by their friend the sun, who wanted them to be sure of their way before leaving them for the night.

But now fear fell upon the children, for the arrows faded, leaving the island in gloom. They had been flying apart, but they huddled close to Peter now. His careless manner was gone too. They were now flying so low that sometimes a tree grazed their feet. Nothing horrid was visible in the air, yet their progress had become slow and labored, exactly as if they were pushing their way through hostile forces. Sometimes Peter had to beat on the air with his fists.

"They don't want us to land," he explained. He did not explain who "they" were. Tinker Bell had been asleep on his shoulder, but now he wakened her and sent her on in front.

Sometimes Peter poised himself in the air, listening with his hand to his ear, and again he would stare down with eyes so bright they seemed to bore two holes to earth. His courage was almost appalling.

"Do you want an adventure?" he said casually to John. "There's a pirate asleep in the pampas just beneath us. If you like we'll go down and kill him."

"Suppose," John said, after a little pause, "he were to wake up."

Peter spoke indignantly. "You don't suppose I would kill him while he was sleeping! I would wake him first, and then kill him. That's the way I always do."

"I say! Do you kill many?"

"I kill tons of them," Peter boasted.

John asked if there were many pirates on the island just now, and Peter said he had never known so many.

"Who is captain now?"

"Hook," answered Peter, and his face became very stern as he said that hated name.

"James Hook?"

"Aye," answered Peter, looking grimmer than ever.

Then Michael began to cry, and even John could speak only in gulps, for he knew Hook's reputation.

"He is the worst of them all," John whispered huskily. "What is he like? Is he big?"

"He is not so big as he was," Peter said.

"How do you mean?"

"I cut off a bit of him."

"You!"

"Yes, me," said Peter sharply.

"But, what bit?"

"His right hand."

"Then he can't fight now?" said John.

"Oh, can't he just!" Peter answered. "He has an iron hook instead of a right hand, and he claws with it."

"Claws!"

"I say, John," said Peter, "there is one thing that every boy who serves under me has to promise, and so must you."

John paled.

"It is this," Peter went on. "If we meet Hook in open fight you must leave him to me."

"I promise," John said loyally.

For the moment they were feeling less scary, because Tink was flying with them, and in her light they could see one another. Unfortunately she could not fly so slowly as they, and so she had to go around and around in a circle. Wendy liked this, but Peter pointed out that the pirates below, seeing her light, would guess they were near the island. The pirates had got out their big gun, Long Tom.

"If only one of us had a pocket," Peter said, "we could carry her in it."

However, they had set out in such a hurry that there was not a pocket among the four of them.

Then Peter had a happy idea. John's hat! Tink agreed to travel by hat, if it was carried in the hand. She had hoped to be carried by Peter. But first John carried the hat, and then Wendy took it, and this led to mischief.

For a while they flew on in silence.

Suddenly the air was rent by a tremendous crash. The pirates had fired Long Tom at them. No one was hit, but Peter was carried by the force of the shot far out to sea, while Wendy was blown upward with no companion but Tinker Bell.

It would have been well for Wendy if at that moment she had dropped the hat, for Tink suddenly popped out of it and began to lure Wendy to her destruction. Tink was not all bad, but at that moment she was full of jealousy of Wendy. What she said in her lovely tinkle Wendy could not of course understand. Some of it was bad, but it sounded kind, and she flew backward and forward, plainly meaning ''Follow me, and all will be well.''

What else could poor Wendy do? She called to Peter and John and Michael and got only mocking echoes in reply. And so, bewildered, and now staggering in her flight, she followed Tink to her doom.

The Island Come True

Feeling that Peter was on his way back, the island had a-wakened into life. In his absence things were usually quiet on the island, but now one had only to put one's ear to the ground to hear the whole island seething with life.

On this evening the chief forces of the island were disposed as follows. The lost boys were out looking for Peter, the pirates were out looking for the lost boys, the Indians were out looking for the pirates, and the beasts were out looking for the Indians. They were going around and around the island, but they did not meet because all were going at the same rate.

All wanted blood except the boys, who were out tonight to greet their captain. There were six of them, counting the twins as two. They were forbidden by Peter to look in the least like him, and they wore the skins of animals slain by themselves. First there was Tootles, who had a kind, sweet nature, and had been in fewer adventures than the others. Then there was Nibs, who was gay and light-hearted, and Slightly, who was the most conceited of the boys. The fourth was Curly, who was always in some trouble or other, and last were the twins, who always kept close together.

The first to fall out of the circle moving around the island were the boys. They flung themselves down on the grass, close to their underground home.

"I do wish Peter would come back," every one of them said nervously.

"I am the only one who is not afraid of the pirates," Slightly said. "But I wish Peter would come back and tell us whether he has heard anything more about Cinderella."

While they talked they heard a distant sound. It was a grim song:

Yo ho, yo ho, the pirate life,
The flag o' skull and bones,
A merry hour, a hempen rope,
And hey for Davy Jones.

At once the lost boys were no longer there. Rabbits could not have disappeared more quickly. With the exception of Nibs, who had darted away to keep watch, they were already in their home under the ground. How had they reached it? On the ground above were seven large trees, each having in its trunk a hole as large as a boy. These were the seven entrances to the home under the ground for which Hook had been searching in vain these many moons.

As the pirates advanced, one, with a quick eye, sighted Nibs disappearing through the woods.

"Shall I go after him, Captain?" the pirate asked.

"Not now," Hook said darkly. "He is only one, and I want to catch all seven. Scatter and look for them."

The men were a villainous-looking lot. In the midst of them, blackest and largest of them all, James Hook lay at his ease in a rough chariot drawn by his men. Instead of a right hand he had the iron hook with which he encouraged them to increase their pace. He was thin and black-visaged, with his hair hanging in long curls which gave him a sinister look. In his mouth he had a holder which enabled him to smoke two cigars at once. But undoubtedly the grimmest part of him was his iron claw. Such was the terrible man against whom Peter Pan was pitted.

Now, as his men fanned out to look for the boys, he seemed moved to talk confidingly with his faithful bosun, Smee.

"Most of all," Hook was saying, "I want their captain, Peter Pan. 'Twas he cut off my arm." He brandished the hook threateningly. "I've waited long to shake his hand with this. Oh, I'll tear him!"

He cast a look of pride upon his iron hand and one of scorn upon the other. Then again he frowned.

"Peter flung my arm," he said, wincing, "to a crocodile that happened to be passing by."

"I have often," said Smee, "noticed your strange dread of crocodiles."

"Not of crocodiles," Hook corrected him, "but of that one crocodile." He lowered his voice. "It liked my arm so much, Smee, that it has followed me ever since, from sea to sea and from land to land, licking its lips for the rest of me."

"In a way," said Smee, "it's a sort of compliment."

"I want no such compliments," Hook barked angrily. "I want Peter Pan, who first gave the brute its taste for me."

He sat down on a large mushroom, and now there was a quiver in his voice. "Smee," he said huskily, "that crocodile would have had me before this, but by a lucky chance it swallowed a clock which goes *tick, tick* inside it, and so before it can reach me I hear the tick and bolt." He laughed, but in a hollow way.

"Some day," said Smee, "the clock will run down, and then he'll get you."

Hook wetted his dry lips. "Aye," he said, "that's the fear that haunts me."

Since sitting down he had felt curiously warm. "Smee," he said, "this seat is hot." He jumped up. He and Smee examined the huge mushroom on which he had been sitting. They tried to pull it up, and it came away at once in their hands, for it had no root. Stranger still, smoke began at once to come up. The pirates looked at each other. "A chimney!" they both exclaimed.

They had indeed discovered the chimney of the home under the ground. Not only smoke came out of it; there came also children's voices. For so safe did the boys feel in their hiding place that they were gaily chattering. The pirates listened grimly and then replaced the mushroom. They looked around them and noted the holes in the seven trees.

"Did you hear them say Peter Pan's away from home?" Smee whispered, fidgeting with his cutlass.

Hook stood for a long time lost in thought, and at last a curdling smile lit up his swarthy face. Smee had been waiting for it. "Unrip your plan, Captain," he cried eagerly.

"To return to the ship," Hook replied slowly through his teeth, "and cook a large rich cake of a jolly thickness with green sugar on it. We will leave the cake where the boys will find it. They will gobble it up because, having no mother, they don't know how dangerous 'tis to eat rich, damp cake." He burst into laughter. "Aha, they will die!"

Smee had listened with growing admiration.

"It's the wickedest, prettiest policy ever I heard of," he cried; and in their exultation the two danced and sang:

> Avast, belay, when I appear,
> By fear they're overtook;
> Nought's left upon your bones when you
> Have shaken claws with Hook.

They began the chorus, but they never finished it, for another sound broke in and stilled them. It was at first a tiny sound, but as it came nearer it was more distinct.

Tick tick tick tick.

Hook stopped dancing, one foot in the air. He shuddered. "The crocodile," he gasped, and bounded away, followed by his bosun.

Now the boys came out once more into the open. Presently Nibs rushed breathless into their midst.

"I have seen a wonderful thing," he cried as they gathered around him eagerly. ''A great white bird. It is flying this way.''

''What kind of a bird, do you think?''

''I don't know,'' Nibs said, ''but it looks so weary, and as it flies it moans, 'poor Wendy.'''

Wendy was now almost overhead, and they could hear her plaintive cry. But more distinct came the shrill voice of Tinker Bell. The jealous fairy had now cast off all disguise of friendship and was darting at her victim from every direction, pinching savagely.

''Hullo, Tink,'' cried the wondering boys.

Tink's reply rang out: ''Peter wants you to shoot the Wendy.''

It was not in their nature to question when Peter ordered.

Tootles had a bow and arrow with him, and Tink noted it. ''Quick, Tootles, quick,'' she screamed. ''Peter will be so pleased.''

Tootles excitedly fitted the arrow to his bow. ''Out of the way, Tink,'' he shouted. Then he fired, and Wendy fluttered to the ground with an arrow in her breast.

"I have shot the Wendy," Tootles cried proudly to the other boys. "Peter will be so pleased with me."

Overhead Tinker Bell laughed and then went into hiding. The others did not hear her. They had crowded around Wendy, and as they looked a terrible silence fell upon the wood.

Slightly was the first to speak. "This is no bird," he said in a scared voice. "I think it must be a lady."

"A lady?" said Tootles, trembling.

"Now I see," Curly said. "Peter was bringing us a lady to take care of us at last, and you have killed her."

Tootles' face was very white. "I must go away," he said, shaking. "I am so afraid of Peter."

It was at this tragic moment that they heard a sound which made the heart of every one of them rise in his mouth. They heard Peter crow.

"Peter!" they cried, for it was always in this way that he signaled his return.

"Hide her," they whispered, and gathered hastily around Wendy. But Tootles stood aloof. Again came that ringing crow, and Peter dropped down in front of them.

"Great news, boys," he cried. "I have brought at last a mother for you all. Have you not seen her? She flew this way."

"Peter," said Tootles quickly, "I will show her to you." To the others he said, "Stand back, let Peter see."

30

So they all stood back, and Peter looked at Wendy. Then he saw the arrow. He took it from her heart and faced his band.

"Whose arrow?" he demanded sternly.

"Mine, Peter," said Tootles, on his knees. Peter raised the arrow to use it as a dagger. Tootles did not flinch. "Strike, Peter," he said.

"I cannot strike," said Peter with awe. "There is something stays my hand."

"It is she," cried Nibs, "the Wendy lady. See, she has raised her arm."

"She lives!" Peter said. Then he knelt beside her and found his button, which she had put on the chain she wore around her neck. "See," he said, "the arrow struck against this. It is the kiss I gave her. It has saved her life."

"Listen to Tink," said Curly. "She is crying because the Wendy lives."

Then they had to tell Peter of Tink's crime, and almost never had they seen him look so stern.

"Listen, Tinker Bell," he cried, "I am your friend no more. Begone from me forever." She flew on his shoulder and pleaded, but he brushed her off. Not until Wendy again raised her arm did he relent sufficiently to say, "Well, not forever, but for a whole week."

But what to do with Wendy in her present delicate state of health?

"Let us carry her down into the house," Curly suggested.

"No, no," Peter said, "you must not touch her. It would not be sufficiently respectful."

"But if she lies there," Tootles said, "she will die."

"Aye," Slightly admitted, "but there is no way out."

"Yes, there is," cried Peter. "Let us build a little house around her."

They were all delighted. "Quick," he ordered them, "bring me, each of you, the best of what we have." In a moment they were scurrying this way and that, down for bedding, up for firewood. And while they were at it, who should appear but John and Michael. Peter had quite forgotten them.

"Curly," said Peter in his most captainy voice, "see that these boys help in the building of the house."

In the meantime the woods had been alive with the sound of axes; almost everything needed for a cozy dwelling already lay at Wendy's feet.

"If only we knew the kind of house she likes best," said one of the boys.

"Peter," shouted another, "she is moving in her sleep. Her mouth opens."

"Perhaps she is going to sing in her sleep," said Peter. "Wendy, sing the kind of house you would like to have."

Immediately, without opening her eyes, Wendy began to sing:

I wish I had a pretty house,
The littlest ever seen,
With funny little red walls,
And roof of mossy green.

By the greatest good luck the branches they had brought were sticky with red sap, and all the ground was carpeted with moss.

When the house was made just as Wendy had asked, Peter strode up and down ordering finishing touches. When it seemed absolutely finished, nothing remained to do but to knock.

The boys stood before the door, trying to look their best. Peter knocked politely.

The door opened, and a lady came out. It was Wendy. They all whipped off their hats.

Slightly was the first to speak. "Wendy lady," he said, "for you we built this house."

"Oh, say you're pleased," cried Nibs.

"Lovely, darling house," Wendy said, and they were the very words the boys had hoped she would say.

Then they all went on their knees and, holding out their arms, cried, ''O Wendy lady, be our mother.''

''Ought I?'' Wendy said, all shining. ''Of course, I am only a little girl, and I have no real experience.''

And then, when they pleaded with her, ''Very well,'' she said, ''I will do my best. Come inside at once, you naughty children; I am sure your feet are damp. And before I put you to bed, I have just time to finish the story of Cinderella.''

By and by she tucked them up in the great bed in the home under the trees, but she herself slept that night in the little house, and Peter kept watch outside with drawn sword, for the pirates could be heard carousing far away and the wolves were on the prowl.

The Home Under the Ground

How they grew to love their home under the ground, especially Wendy! It consisted of one large room with a floor in which you could dig, and in this floor grew stout mushrooms which were used as stools. A Never tree tried hard to grow in the center of the room, but every morning the boys sawed the trunk through, level with the floor. By evening it was always about two feet high, and then they put a board on top of it, making it a table. As soon as the meal was cleared away, they sawed off the trunk again, and then there was more room to play. There was an enormous fireplace, and across this Wendy stretched strings from which she suspended her washing. The bed was tilted against the wall by day and let down at six thirty, when it filled nearly half the room, and all the boys except Michael slept in it. Wendy had to have a baby, so Michael, being the littlest, was hung up in a basket.

There was one recess in the wall, no larger than a bird cage, which was the private apartment of Tinker Bell. It could be shut off from the rest of the home by a tiny curtain.

It was all especially entrancing to Wendy because those rampageous boys of hers gave her so much to do. The cooking kept her nose to the pot, and there were whole weeks when she was never above ground except on an occasional evening when she did her mending. Wendy's favorite time for sewing and darning was after the boys had all gone to bed.

As time wore on, did Wendy think much about the beloved

35

parents she had left behind? Perhaps, but she did not really worry about them. She was sure they would always keep the window open for her to fly back. What did disturb her at times was that John remembered his parents only vaguely, as people he had once known, and Michael was quite willing to believe that she was really his mother. These things scared her a little, and she tried to keep them remembering the old life.

When Peter was home, he would help Wendy manage the children. But he was never really happy about pretending to be their father. Once he asked anxiously, "It is only make-believe, isn't it? It would make me seem so old to be their father. I'm not really, Wendy?"

"Not if you don't wish it," Wendy answered him. Then she asked firmly, "Peter, what are your exact feelings toward me?"

"Those of a devoted son, Wendy."

"I thought so," she said, and went and sat by herself at the extreme end of the room.

"You are so queer," said Peter, puzzled.

Then came the evening which, though none of them knew it, was to be the last in their underground home. The day had been almost uneventful, and now the children were having their evening meal.

Above, the Indians were on guard. Tiger Lily, their beautiful princess, had once been saved by Peter from a dreadful fate at the hands of the pirates. Ever since, there was nothing she and her braves would not do for him. All night they would sit keeping watch over the home underground, awaiting the attack by the pirates that was sure to come.

The children were playing noisily when Wendy heard Peter's step above.

"Children, I hear your father's step," she said. "He likes you to meet him at the door."

Now they heard the Indians greet Peter. "Watch well, braves," Peter said as he passed them and began his descent through the tree.

Then, as so often before, the gay children rushed to drag Peter in. As so often before, but never again!

Now it was time for Wendy's good-night story, the story they loved best; the story Peter hated. Usually when she began to tell this story he left the room, but tonight he remained on his stool.

Wendy's Story

"Listen, then," said Wendy, settling down to her story with Michael at her feet and seven boys in the bed. "There was once a gentleman—"

"I had rather he had been a lady," Curly said.

"Quiet," their mother scolded. "There was a lady also. The gentleman's name was Mr. Darling, and her name was Mrs. Darling."

"I knew them," John said, to annoy the others.

"I think I knew them," Michael said rather doubtfully.

"They were married," Wendy went on, "and what do you think they had?"

"White rats," cried Nibs, inspired.

"No! They had three children," said Wendy. "Now these three children had a faithful nurse called Nana, but Mr. Darling was angry with her and chained her up in the yard. And so all the children flew away. They flew away to the Neverland, where the lost children are."

"Oh, Wendy," cried Tootles, "was one of the lost children called Tootles?"

"Hush! Now I want you to consider the feelings of the unhappy parents with all their children flown away. Think of the empty beds!"

"I don't see how it can have a happy ending," said the second twin.

"Have no fear," said Wendy. She had now come to the part that Peter hated. "You see," she went on, "the children knew that the mother would always leave the window open for them to fly back by, so they stayed away for years and had a lovely time. And when they were quite grown up they went back, and there was the window still standing open. So up they flew to their mummy and daddy, and pen cannot describe the happy scene.''

When Wendy finished, Peter uttered a hollow groan.

''What is it, Peter?'' she cried, running to him.

''Wendy, you are wrong about mothers.'' And now he told what he had previously concealed.

''Long ago,'' he said, ''I thought like you that my mother would always keep the window open for me, so I stayed away for moons and moons and moons, and then flew back. But the window was barred, and there was another little boy sleeping in my bed.''

''Wendy, let us go home,'' cried John and Michael together.

''Yes,'' she said, clutching them.

''Not tonight?'' asked the lost boys, bewildered.

''At once,'' said Wendy resolutely. ''Peter, will you make the necessary arrangements?''

''If you wish it,'' he replied coolly. If she did not mind parting, he was going to show her that neither did he! But of course, he cared very much and was full of wrath against grownups, who, as usual, were spoiling everything.

''Tinker Bell will take you across the sea,'' he said in a short, sharp voice. ''Wake her, Nibs.''

Now Wendy saw that the boys were gazing very forlornly at her, and her heart melted.

''Dear ones,'' she said, ''if you will all come home with me I feel almost sure I can get my father and mother to adopt you.''

The boys jumped for joy. ''Peter, can we go?'' they all cried.

''All right,'' Peter replied with a bitter smile, and immediately they rushed to get their things.

''And now, Peter,'' Wendy said, thinking she had put everything right, ''I am going to give you your medicine before you go.'' But then she saw a look on Peter's face that made her heart sink.

"I am not going with you, Wendy," he said.

"To find your mother," she coaxed.

"No!" he told Wendy. "Perhaps she would say I was old, and I just want always to be a little boy and to have fun."

And so the others had to be told. "Peter isn't coming."

Peter not coming! They gazed blankly at him, their sticks over their backs, and on each stick a bundle.

"Now then," cried Peter, "no fuss, no blubbering. Good-bye, Wendy," and he held out his hand cheerily. She had to take his hand, as there was no indication that he would prefer a thimble.

"You will remember to take your medicine, Peter?"

"Yes."

That seemed to be everything, and an awkward pause followed. Peter, however, was not the kind who breaks down before people. "Are you ready, Tinker Bell?" he called out.

"Aye, aye."

"Then lead the way."

Tink darted up the nearest tree, but no one followed her, for it was at this moment that the pirates made their dreadful attack upon the Indians. Above, where all had been so still, the air was rent with shrieks and the clash of steel. Below, there was dead silence. Peter seized his sword, and the lust of battle was in his eye.

The Children Are Carried Off

The pirate attack had taken the Indians by surprise. Around the brave Tiger Lily were a dozen of her stoutest warriors. Suddenly, without warning, they saw the pirates bearing down on them, and they seized their weapons. The air was torn with the war cry. But it was too late. Many were slain, and only Tiger Lily and a small remnant of her tribe escaped through the dark woods.

But for the victorious Hook the night's work was not yet over. It was not the Indians he had come to destroy. It was Peter Pan he wanted, Peter and Wendy and their band, but chiefly Peter.

In the meantime the boys waited below to know their fate. Which side had won? The pirates, listening at the mouths of the trees, heard this question put by every boy, and, alas, they also heard Peter's answer.

"If the Indians have won," he said, "they will beat the tom-tom. It is always their sign of victory."

Now, Smee had found the tom-tom, and was at that moment sitting on it. To his amazement Hook signed to him to beat the tom-tom, and slowly there came to Smee an understanding of the dreadful wickedness of the order. Twice Smee beat upon the instrument, and then stopped to listen.

"The tom-tom," the pirates heard Peter cry. "An Indian victory!"

The children answered with a cheer that was music to the black hearts above. They repeated their good-byes to Peter. Rapidly and silently Hook gave his orders: one man to each tree, and the others to arrange themselves in a line two yards apart.

The first to emerge from his tree was Curly. He rose out of it into the arms of one of the pirates, who flung him to another, and then to another, and so he was tossed from one to another until he fell at the feet of the black pirate. All of the boys were plucked and tossed in this ruthless manner, like bales of goods flung from hand to hand.

A different treatment was accorded to Wendy, who came last. With ironical politeness Hook raised his hat to her and, offering her his arm, escorted her to the spot where the others were being gagged and tied to prevent their flying away.

Hook now signed to his men that the captives were to be taken to the ship. The little house was to be used as a conveyance. The children were flung into it, four stout pirates raised it on their shoulders, the others fell in behind, and singing the hateful pirate chorus the strange procession set off through the woods.

Now Hook was alone. He tiptoed to one of the trees. Intently he listened for any sound from below. Was Peter asleep? Or did he stand waiting at the foot of the tree with his dagger in his hand?

There was no way of knowing except by going down. Hook was a brave man, but for a moment he had to stop and wipe his brow, which was dripping like a candle. Then silently he let himself go down into the unknown.

He arrived at the foot of the shaft, and as his eyes became accustomed to the dim light, the only thing on which his greedy gaze rested—long sought for and found at last—was the great bed. On the bed lay Peter fast asleep.

Unaware of the tragedy being enacted above, Peter had, after the children left, played gaily on his pipes to prove to himself that he did not care. Then he decided not to take his medicine, so as to grieve Wendy. Then he lay down on the bed. He nearly cried, but it struck him how indignant Wendy would be if he laughed instead, so he laughed a haughty laugh and fell asleep in the middle of it.

In this way—defenseless—Hook found him. He stood silent at the foot of the tree, looking through a small opening. There across the chamber was his enemy. He made a stealthy step but found the way blocked by a low door in the tree. Feeling for the catch, he found to his fury that it was beyond his reach. Was his enemy to escape him after all?

But what was that? The red in his eye had caught sight of Peter's medicine standing on a ledge within easy reach. Immediately he knew that the sleeper was in his power.

For fear that he be taken alive, Hook always carried about his person a dreadful poison, blended by himself. Five drops of this he now added to Peter's medicine. Then one long gloating look he cast upon his victim and, turning, wormed his way up the tree. Now, muttering strangely to himself, he stole away through the woods.

Peter slept on. It must have been not less than ten o'clock by the crocodile when he suddenly sat up in his bed, awakened by a soft tapping on the door of his tree. Peter felt for his dagger till his hand gripped it. Then he spoke. "Who is that?"

"Let me in, Peter."

It was Tink, and quickly he unbarred the door. She flew in excitedly, her face flushed and her dress stained with mud.

"What is it? Out with it!" Peter shouted, and she told him about the capture of Wendy and the boys.

Wendy bound, and on the pirate ship! "I'll rescue her," Peter cried, leaping for his weapons. He thought of something he could do to please her. He would take his medicine.

His hand closed on the fatal draught.

"No!" shrieked Tinker Bell, who had heard Hook muttering about his deed as he sped through the forest. "It is poisoned!"

"Poisoned? Who could have poisoned it?" Peter asked.

"Hook," replied Tinker Bell.

"Don't be silly. How could Hook have got down here? Besides, I never fell asleep." And Peter really believed this.

He raised the cup. Tink knew there was no time for words now; it was time for deeds. With one of her lightning movements she got between Peter's lips and the draught and drained it to the dregs.

"It was poisoned, Peter," she told him softly, "and now I am going to die."

"Oh, Tink, did you drink it to save me?"

"Yes."

Already she was reeling in the air. Her wings could hardly carry her now. She lighted on Peter's shoulder and gave his chin a loving bite. Then, tottering to her chamber, she lay down on the bed.

Peter knelt beside her in distress. Every moment her light was growing fainter, and he knew that if it went out she would be no more. Her voice was so low that at first he could not make out what she said. Then he made it out. She was saying that she thought she could get well again if children believed in fairies.

Peter flung out his arms. There were no children there, and it was nighttime. But he called to all the boys and girls who might be dreaming of the Neverland: "Do you believe?" he cried.

Tink sat up in bed to listen to her fate.

"If you believe," Peter shouted to them, "clap your hands. Don't let Tink die."

Many clapped. Then the clapping stopped suddenly, as if countless mothers had rushed to their nurseries to see what on earth was happening. But already Tink was saved. First her voice grew strong, then she popped out of bed and was flashing through the room.

48

"And now to rescue Wendy," said Peter.

The moon was riding in a cloudy heaven when Peter rose from his tree, his weapons strapped to his side, to set out upon his perilous quest. As he pressed through the silent forest he swore this terrible oath: "Hook or me this time!"

The Pirate Ship

One green light squinting over Kidd's Creek, near the mouth of the pirate river, marked where the brig, the *Jolly Roger,* lay low in the water. A few of the pirates leaned over the bulwarks; others sprawled about the deck.

Hook trod the deck in thought. It was his hour of triumph. Peter had been removed forever from his path—so he thought—and all the other boys were on the brig, about to walk the plank.

"Are all the children chained, so that they cannot fly away?" he shouted.

"Aye, aye," his men answered him.

"Then hoist them up."

The wretched prisoners were dragged from the hold, all except Wendy, and ranged in line in front of him.

"Now then, bullies," he said briskly, "six of you walk the plank tonight, but I have room for two cabin boys. Which of you is it to be?"

When all of the boys refused, Hook roared out, "That seals your doom. Bring up their mother. Get the plank ready."

They were only boys, and they went white as they saw two of the pirates preparing the fatal plank. But they tried to look brave when Wendy was brought up.

"Tie her up," Hook shouted.

He took a step toward Wendy. His intention was to turn her face so that she would see the boys walking the plank one by one. But he never reached her, never heard the cry of anguish he had hoped to

50

wring from her. He heard something else instead. It was the terrible *tick-tick* of the crocodile.

They all heard it, and immediately every head was turned toward Hook. Very frightful it was to see the change that came over him. It was as if he had been clipped at every joint. He fell in a little heap.

"Hide me," he cried hoarsely.

The pirates gathered round him, all eyes averted from the Thing that was coming aboard. They had no thought of fighting it. It was Fate.

Only when Hook was hidden from them did the boys rush to the ship's side to see the crocodile climbing it. Then they got the strangest surprise of this Night of Nights, for it was no crocodile that was coming to their aid. It was Peter!

He signed to them not to make any cry that might arouse suspicion. Then he went on ticking.

"Hook or Me This Time"

Now Peter, his dagger in his hand, scaled the side of the brig as noiselessly as a mouse. He was amazed to see the pirates cowering from him, with Hook in their midst as if he had heard the crocodile. "How clever of me," he thought.

It was at this moment that the quartermaster emerged from the forecastle and came along the deck. Peter struck true and deep. John clapped his hands on the ill-fated pirate's mouth to stifle the dying groan. The man fell forward, and four boys caught him to prevent the thud. Then Peter gave the signal, and the body was cast overboard. There was a splash, and then silence.

None too soon Peter, every inch of him on tiptoe, vanished into the cabin, for more than one private was screwing up his courage to look around.

"It's gone, Captain," Smee said. "All's still again."

Slowly Hook let his head emerge from his ruff and listened intently. There was not a sound, and he drew himself up firmly to his full height. "Then here's to Johnny Plank," he cried, hating the boys more than ever because they had seen him unbend. "Fetch the cat, Jukes. It's in the cabin."

The cabin! Peter was in the cabin. The children gazed at one another.

"Aye, aye," said Jukes blithely, and he strode into the cabin. They followed him with their eyes while Hook began to sing:

What was the last line will never be known, for suddenly the song was stayed by a dreadful screech from the cabin. Then there was a crowing sound which was well understood by the boys, but to the pirates was almost worse than the screech.

"What was that?" cried Hook. The pirate named Cecco hesitated for a moment and then swung into the cabin. At once he tottered out, haggard.

"What's the matter with Bill Jukes, you dog?" hissed Hook.

"The matter with him is he's dead, stabbed," replied Cecco in a hollow voice. "The cabin's black as a pit, but there's something terrible in there—the thing you heard crowing."

"Cecco," said Hook in his steeliest voice, "go back and fetch me out that doodle-doo."

Cecco, bravest of the brave, cowered before his captain, crying, "No, no!" But Hook was purring to his claw.

"Did you say you would go, Cecco?" he said. Cecco went. There was no more singing; all listened now. And again came a death-screech and again a crow.

"'Sdeath and odds fish," thundered Hook, "who is to bring me that doodle-doo?" But none of the crew would go.

Seizing a lantern and raising his claw with a menacing gesture, Hook shouted, "I'll bring out that doodle-doo myself," and he sped into the cabin. In a moment he came staggering out, without his lantern.

"Something blew out the light," he said unsteadily.

"What of Cecco?" demanded a pirate named Noodler.

"He's as dead as Jukes," said Hook shortly.

One after another the men took up the cry, "The ship's doomed!" At this the children could not resist raising a cheer. Hook had forgotten his prisoners, but now his face lit up again.

"Lads," he cried to his crew, "open the cabin door and drive them in. Let them fight the doodle-doo. If they kill him, we're that much better off. If he kills them, we're none the worse."

For the first time his men admired Hook, and devotedly they did his bidding. The boys, pretending to struggle, were pushed into the cabin, and the door was closed on them.

"Now, listen," cried Hook, and all listened. But not one dared to face the door. Yes, one: Wendy, who all this time had been bound to the mast. But it was for neither a scream nor a crow that she was waiting. It was for the reappearance of Peter.

She had not long to wait. In the cabin he had found the thing for which he had gone in search: the key that would free the children of their manacles. And now they all stole forth, armed with such weapons as they could find. First signing to them to hide, Peter cut Wendy's bonds, and then nothing could have been easier than for them all to fly off together. But one thing barred the way: Peter's oath, "Hook or me this time." So when he had freed Wendy he whispered to her to conceal herself with the others, and himself took her place by the mast, her cloak around him so that he should pass for her. Then he took a great breath and crowed.

To the pirates it was a voice crying that all the boys lay slain in the cabin, and they were panic-stricken.

"Lads," cried Hook now, "I've thought it out. There's a Jonah aboard."

"Aye," they snarled, "a man with a hook."

"No, lads, no, it's the girl. Never was luck on a pirate ship with a woman aboard. Fling the girl overboard," cried Hook.

The men rushed at the figure in the cloak. "There's none can save you now, missy," they jeered.

"There's one," replied the figure.

"Who's that?"

"Peter Pan, the avenger!" came the terrible answer, and as he spoke Peter flung off his cloak. "Down, boys, and at them," Peter's voice rang out, and in another moment the clash of arms was resounding through the ship. Had the pirates kept together they might have won. But they were all unstrung, and ran hither and thither, each thinking himself the last survivor of the crew. Some of them leaped into the sea. Others hid in the dark, only to fall easy prey to the swords of the boys.

All were gone when a group of boys surrounded Hook, who seemed to have a charmed life. They had conquered his men, but this man alone seemed to be a match for them all.

Suddenly another sprang into the fray.

"Put up your swords, boys," cried the newcomer, brandishing his sword in a commanding manner. "This man is mine."

Suddenly Hook found himself face to face with Peter. The others drew back and formed a ring around them.

"Proud and insolent youth," said Hook, "prepare to meet thy doom."

"Dark and sinister man," Peter answered, "have at thee."

Without words they fell to, and for a space there was no advantage to either. Peter was a superb swordsman, but his shorter reach stood him in ill stead. Yet, though Hook kept forcing him back, the pirate could not get the better of him. Suddenly the sword fell from Hook's hand, and he was at Peter's mercy.

"Now!" cried all the boys. But with a magnificent gesture Peter invited Hook to pick up his sword.

"Pan, who and what art thou?" Hook cried huskily.

"I'm youth, I'm joy," Peter answered. "I'm a little bird that has broken out of the egg."

This, of course, was nonsense, but it made Hook more unhappy than ever. He fought like a human flail, but Peter fluttered around him, and again and again he darted in and pricked.

Hook was fighting now without hope. Abandoning the fight, he rushed into the room where the gunpowder was stored, and fired it.

"In two minutes," he cried, "the ship will be blown to pieces." But Peter ran from the powder magazine with the shell in his hands and calmly flung it overboard.

Seeing Peter slowly advancing upon him through the air with dagger poised, Hook sprang upon the bulwarks to cast himself into the sea. He did not know that the crocodile was waiting for him, for the clock inside the crocodile had stopped. As the black pirate stood on the bulwark looking over his shoulder, Peter glided through the air and pushed him off with his foot. Thus perished James Hook.

Then the boys took over the ship. A few sharp orders were given by Captain Pan, and they turned the ship around and nosed her for the mainland.

The Return Home

Meantime, what was happening in that desolate home from which the three children took such heartless flight so long ago?

On that eventful evening to which we have now come, Mrs. Darling was in the night-nursery awaiting her husband's return home. She had fallen asleep in her chair. Suddenly she started up, calling the children's names, but there was no one in the room but Nana.

"Oh, Nana, I dreamed my dear ones had come back."

Nana had filmy eyes, but all she could do was to put her paw gently in her mistress's lap. They were sitting thus when Mr. Darling came home from the office. He was tired.

"Won't you play me to sleep on the nursery piano?" he asked. And as Mrs. Darling was crossing to the day-nursery he added thoughtlessly, "And shut that window. I feel a draft."

"Oh, George, never ask me to do that. The window must be left open for them always, always."

He begged her pardon, and she went into the day-nursery and played, and soon Mr. Darling was asleep. While he slept, Peter flew into the room with Tinker Bell.

"Quick, Tink," he whispered, "close the window; bar it. That's right. Now you and I must get away by the door, and when Wendy comes she will think her mother has barred her out, and she will have to come back with me."

Then he peeped into the day-nursery to see who was playing. He whispered to Tink, "It's Wendy's mother."

He did not know the tune, which was "Home, Sweet Home," but he knew it was saying, "Come home, Wendy, Wendy, Wendy," and he cried, "You will never see Wendy again, lady, for the window is barred."

He peeped in again to see why the music had stopped, and now he saw that Mrs. Darling had laid her head on her arm, and that two tears were sitting in her eyes.

"She wants me to unbar the window," thought Peter. "She's awfully fond of Wendy." Then, after a pause, "I'm fond of her too. We can't both have her, lady."

He ceased to look at her, but even then she would not let go of him. It was just as if she were inside him, knocking.

"Oh, all right," he said at last, and gulped. Then he unbarred the window. "Come on, Tink," he cried. "We don't want any silly mothers." And he flew away.

So Wendy and John and Michael found the window open for them after all. They alighted on the floor and looked about. It was then that Mrs. Darling began playing again.

"It's Mother!" cried Wendy, peeping.

"Let us creep in," John suggested, "and put our hands over her eyes." But Wendy, who saw that they must break the joyous news more gently, had a better plan.

"Let us all slip into our beds and be there when she comes in, just as if we had never been away."

And so, when Mrs. Darling went back to the night-nursery to see if her husband was asleep, all the beds were occupied. The children waited for her cry of joy, but it did not come. She saw them, but then, she saw them in their beds so often in her dreams that she thought this was just the dream still. She sat down in the chair by the fire, where in the old days she had nursed them.

"Mother!" Wendy cried.

"That's Wendy," she said, but still she was sure it was the dream.

"Mother!"

"That's John," she said.

"Mother!" cried Michael. He knew her now.

"That's Michael," she said, and she stretched out her arms for the three children they would never envelop again. Yes, they did! They went around Wendy and John and Michael, who had slipped out of bed and run to her.

"George, George," she cried when she could speak, and Mr. Darling woke to share her bliss, and Nana came rushing in. There could not have been a lovelier sight—but there was none to see it except a

strange boy who was staring in at the window. He had ecstasies innumerable that other children can never know, but he was looking through the window at the one joy from which he must forever be barred.

The six boys had been waiting below to give Wendy time to explain about them. When they went up, Mrs. Darling said at once that she would have them, though Mr. Darling did think six a rather large number. Somehow they were all fitted in.

As for Peter, he saw Wendy once again before he flew away. He did not exactly come to the window, but he brushed against it in passing, so that she could open it if she liked and call to him. That was what she did.

"Hullo, Wendy, good-bye," he said.

"Oh dear, are you going away?" Wendy asked.

"Yes."

Mrs. Darling came to the window, for she was keeping a sharp eye on Wendy. She told Peter that she had adopted all the other boys and would like to adopt him too.

"No," said Peter. "I don't want to go to school and learn solemn things. I don't want to be a man. I want always to be a boy and have fun."

"But where are you going to live?" Mrs. Darling asked him.

"With Tink in the house we built for Wendy. The fairies are going to put it high up among the treetops where they sleep at night."

"It will be rather lonely in the evening," said Wendy.

Mrs. Darling saw his mouth twitch, and she made him this offer: she would let Wendy go to him for a week every year to do his spring cleaning. This promise sent Peter away quite gay again.

"You won't forget me, Peter, will you?" Wendy called to him. Peter promised, and then he flew away.